THE BRAND-NEW, NEVER-USED, PERFECT CRAYONS

LEANNE HATCH

MARGARET FERGUSON BOOKS
HOLIDAY HOUSE · NEW YORK

FOR MOM AND DAD

Margaret Ferguson Books

Text and illustrations copyright © 2023 by Leanne Hatch

All Rights Reserved

HOLIDAY HOUSE is registered in the U.S. Patent and Trademark Office.

Printed and bound in April 2023 at C&C Offset, Shenzhen, China.

The artwork was created digitally.

www.holidayhouse.com

First Edition

1 3 5 7 9 10 8 6 4 2

Library of Congress Cataloging-in-Publication Data

Names: Hatch, Leanne, author, illustrator.

Title: The brand-new, never-used, perfect crayons / Leanne Hatch.

Description: First edition. | New York : Holiday House, [2023]

"Margaret Ferguson Books." | Audience: Ages 4 to 8. | Audience: Grades K–1.

Summary: "When Violet gets a super big box of crayons she can't bring

herself to use them because they are so perfect"— Provided by publisher.

Identifiers: LCCN 2022018005 | ISBN 9780823452309 (hardcover)

Subjects: LCSH: Crayons—Juvenile fiction. | Sisters—Juvenile fiction.

CYAC: Crayons—Fiction. | Sisters—Fiction. | LCGFT: Picture books.

Classification: LCC PZ7.1.H3798 Br 2023 | DDC [E]—dc23

LC record available at https://lccn.loc.gov/2022018005

ISBN: 978-0-8234-5230-9 (hardcover)

Violet was in the art supply aisle when she first spotted them. There were small boxes, medium boxes, big boxes, and . . .

The super big box of crayons had all the colors
she would ever need. Eighty-four to be exact.

Violet imagined all the wonderful things
she could draw with that many colors.

Dad made her a deal.

That afternoon, after Violet
had finished feeding the cat,

taking out the recycling,

and sweeping up the crumbs that her sister
Marigold had dropped, she went to her bedroom.

Violet could not wait to get started.

She got out her sketch pad and carefully emptied
out the box of brand-new, never-used crayons.

All the crayons were matching in length, perfectly pointed, and had smooth, uniform wrappers. And those colors! All eighty-four of them.

There was even one with her name on it.

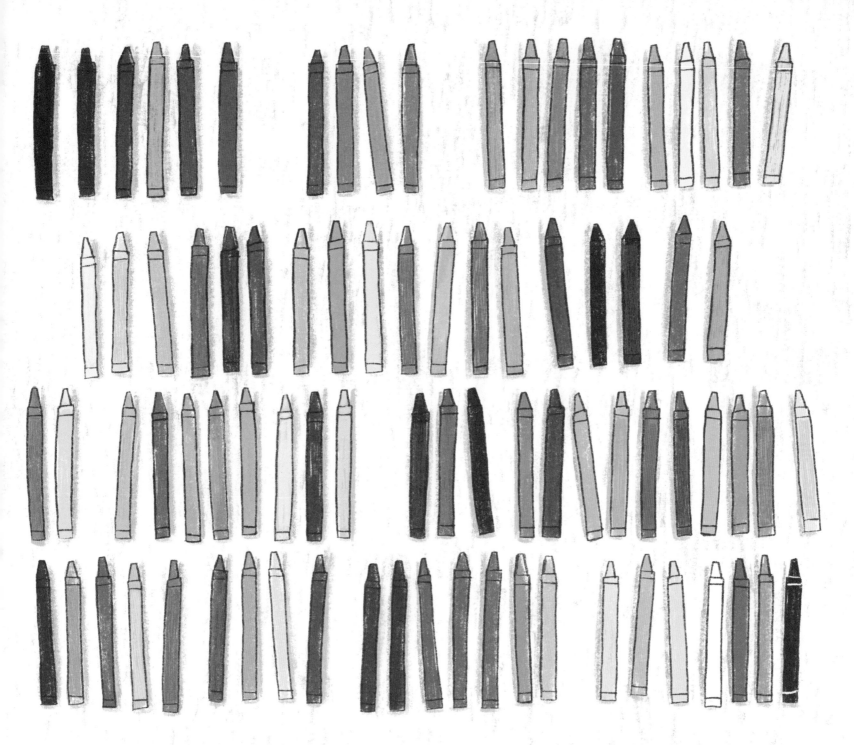

First Violet arranged them by shade.

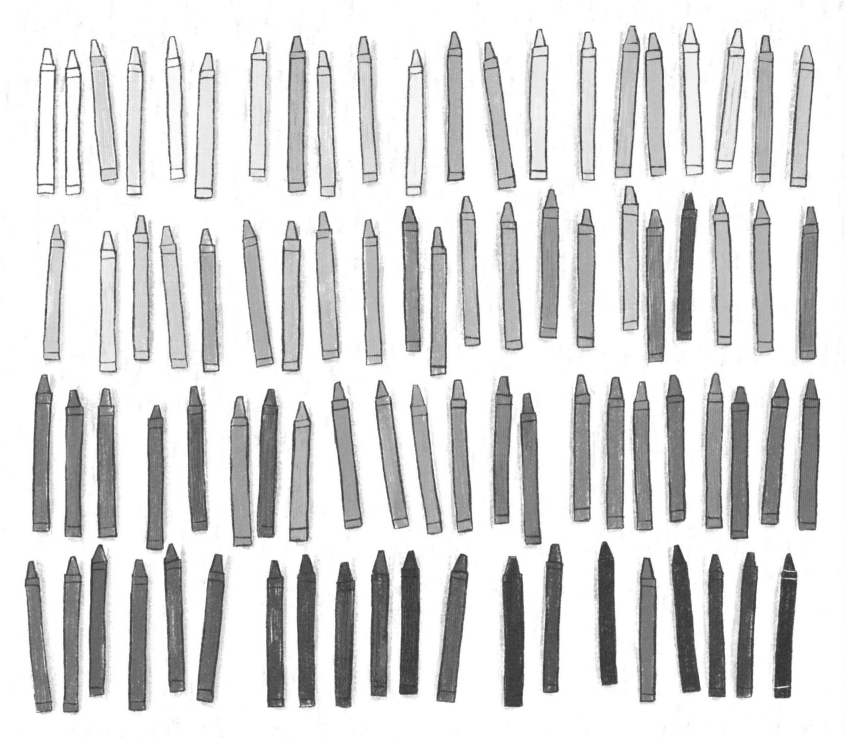

Then from light to dark.

"Why aren't you drawing?" Marigold asked.

"They are too pretty. I don't want to ruin them," Violet said.

"I think I'll save them for another day."

She put them back in their box and placed them on her desk.

But she couldn't bring herself to use them the next day.

Or the day after that.

Marigold admired them when Violet wasn't looking.

Marigold asked if she could use Violet's crayons.

"No," said Violet. "I want my crayons to stay nice.
You can use the old ones."

The old crayons were in a shoebox, broken and flat, with torn wrappers. There weren't anywhere near eighty-four colors.

Violet found them uninspiring.

But not Marigold.

She decorated her paper with bright swirls
and bold waves. She layered colors over
other colors. She made thick lines and thin lines.

Violet thought it was a mess.

"There's beauty in imperfection," said Mom.

Violet disagreed. Beauty is found
in a super big box of brand-new,
never-used, perfect crayons.

When Marigold ran
out of blank paper,
she left to get more.

Violet began to wonder what was taking so long.

"What are you doing?"
cried Violet.

"I'm making you a drawing,"
said Marigold.

Violet sent Marigold away. She wanted to be alone.

At first, Violet was angry with her sister.
Then she was angry at the crayons.

She was tired of worrying about them.

Minutes later, she heard a soft knock
on her door.

Marigold brought Violet the
drawing she had made for her.
She was sorry for getting into her things.

Violet was sorry for getting angry.

Violet knew just what to do to make things better.

And together, they wore down the perfectly pointed tips
of eighty-four brand-new, never-used, perfect crayons.